OUR LITTLE MACEDONIAN COUSIN OF LONG AGO

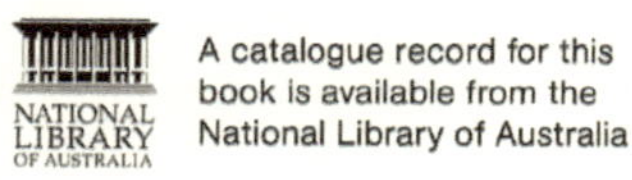
NATIONAL
LIBRARY
OF AUSTRALIA
A catalogue record for this
book is available from the
National Library of Australia

OUR LITTLE MACEDONIAN COUSIN OF LONG AGO

by

Julia Darrow Cowles

CONTENTS

Nearchus

PREFACE

THE author of "Our Little Macedonian Cousin of Long Ago," has not attempted to write history in her story. She has sought, rather, to sketch a background of Macedonian lights and shadows, trusting that, when the readers of the story begin their study of the lives of Philip of Macedon and Alexander the Great, the details of literal history may—against this background—stand out with greater reality.

The typical life of a Macedonian boy attached to the court of Philip is portrayed, however, in true accord with the spirit and trend of Macedonian history.

PRONUNCIATION OF PROPER NAMES

A-chil'les (a-kil'lēz)
A-da
Ae-ge'an
Aes'chi-nes
Al-ex-an'der
A-myn'tas
An-tip'a-ter
A-pel'lēs
A-re'tis
Ar-is-tot'le (tot'l)
A-the'ni-ans
At'ta-lus
Bu-ceph'a-lus
Cha'ri-tas
Co-rin'thi-ans
Di'a-des
Greeks
Har-pa'lus
Her-mes'
Il'i-ad
Lao'di-ce
Le-on'i-das
Lu'di-as
Ly-sim'a-chus
Ly-sip'pus
Mac'e-don
Mac'e-do'ni-a
Med'i-ter-ra'ne-an
Mez'za
Ne-ar'chus
O'drys
O-dys-sey

O-lyn'thi-a
O-lyn'thus
O-lym'pi-a
O-lym'pic
O-lym'pus
Par-me'ni-on
Pe'leus or pee'lūs
Pel'la
Phil'ip
Phi-lol'tas
Phoe'nix (fee'niks)
Pin'dar
Ptol-e-my (tol'eme)
Spar'tan
Sta-gei'ra
Thes'sa-ly

CHAPTER I

LEAVING HOME

"**A**RT ready, lad?"

"Yes, father."

"'Tis time we were on our way."

The young boy addressed turned to his mother and kissed her once more. Then, saying a last farewell to his younger brother and sister, he mounted the horse which stood beside that of his father. Together they rode down the path that led from their home, close to the foothills which surrounded the plain of Macedonia.

If the mother found it hard to see her older son leaving home she showed no sign, but waved a last good-by as he turned at the bend of the path that shut him away from her sight.

Every Macedonian mother of the higher classes looked forward to the time when her son should go to the court of King Philip, at Pella, and there serve as a Page, while being educated for a life of devotion to his country. So the natural sorrow of parting was softened by the honor and advancement awaiting the boy.

"And will I go, too, in a few years?" asked Diades, the younger boy, as they turned back into the house.

"Yes," replied his mother, "you will go, too, when you are as old as Nearchus. Your father is a Companion of the King, you know, and the sons of all the Companions are educated at court."

"When I am as old as Nearchus," repeated Diades. "That will be in three years. Oh, what a long time!"

"Does it seem long?" smiled his mother. "It does not seem long to me," and she drew the little fellow to her in a quick embrace.

"I will stay," cried Ada, running to share the embrace.

"Yes, you will stay and be my companion," said her mother, kissing the rosy, upturned face.

In the meantime Nearchus and his father rode rapidly on. Parmenion looked forward with pride and joy to the moment when he should present his son to the King, Philip of Macedon, and say, "My lord, this is Nearchus, my son. May he serve you well."

Parmenion was proud of his boy, as he had a right to be, for Nearchus was well built, rugged, yet lithe of limb, and with regular features and a clear skin. His life had been free and wild. He had played, as all boys play, at games and sports of various sorts which had developed his muscles and tested his endurance. He had hunted the small animals of the foothills near his home and had bathed in the cold waters of the river.

Of lessons he had had none. Schools were unknown in Macedonia, and except in rare instances the boys who came to the court of the King had had little or nothing of what could be termed an education.

Nearchus' speech was the Macedonian dialect spoken by the common people. His father, Parmenion, spoke Greek, which he had learned at the court of Philip, and Nearchus had picked up a few Greek words. But Parmenion was seldom at home, so he had learned but little from him.

As Nearchus rode on by his father's side, his mind was in a tumult. At last the day had come: the day he had looked forward to ever since he could remember, when he should be taken to court! It seemed strange — yes, and a little hard, too — that he was never to return to his old life of the hills and the plain, for he loved the freedom of it; but a look ahead made him forget all that. He would be a Page of the King. He would wait upon the King, serve him, and be taught the ways of the King's court.

He looked up at his father, and in mind he contrasted him with the rude men of the hill country beyond his home. He was proud of his father; of his manly bearing, his erect carriage, his softly flowing speech, but most of all, of his courage and loyalty to the King.

Then a sudden shyness came over the boy, as he thought of the new companions he was to meet. "I wonder if they will laugh at my rough dialect," he questioned. Then he remembered that they, too, must have spoken the same before they served the King. "And perhaps there will be others just learning," he added to himself, by way of encouragement.

Presently his father turned to him. "You will have many companions at Pella," he said, "and you will not be the elder brother there. You must learn to give and take with the others; be quick and ready in your service to the King; and study your lessons faithfully. Be generous, be true, and be brave, just as you have been at home. Then you will have friends among the boys, and I shall have cause to be proud of you."

"Do you know any of the boys at the court?" asked Nearchus after a pause.

"Not well," replied Parmenion. "But Alexander, the son of Philip, must be close to your age. I trust that you and he may be friends."

Nearchus' cheeks flushed. His father had spoken to him of Alexander before; of the boy's singular beauty, his soldierly bearing, and of his frank and generous nature.

Nearchus had thought much about him, for as son of the King he was already a hero in his eyes. In truth, he had dreamed of him more than once, as the time drew near for his own entrance to the court. But never had he dared to think of Alexander as his friend!

When Parmenion looked at Nearchus again there was a deeper flush on the boy's cheeks and a new sparkle in his eyes.

"See," said Parmenion, pointing ahead, as they made a turn in the road, and Nearchus, glancing quickly up, saw at a distance the stone walls which surrounded the city of Pella.

A few moments more and they had entered the gates, and Nearchus looked eagerly about him.

The city was built upon the shore of a sparkling lake, Lake Ludias; and the houses were dotted here and there with little order or regularity, for the streets were little more than winding paths.

Ahead of them rose the great walls of the King's palace, and Nearchus' breath came quickly as he looked at those formidable walls and wondered what the life within them would be.

CHAPTER II
NEARCHUS BECOMES A PAGE

As they drew near to the outer gates of the palace, they met a group of boys accompanied by an older man.

"They are doubtless going to the school or the gymnasium," said Parmenion, and he exchanged a word of greeting with the man. "That is Leonidas," he added. "He is a relative of Queen Olympia, and has charge of Alexander's education."

"Is Alexander among them?" asked Nearchus eagerly.

"No," replied Parmenion, "I do not see him."

Nearchus scanned eagerly the faces of the boys who passed him, and they in turn looked curiously at him.

"A new Page," he heard one of them say. "I wonder what he will be like."

As they were about to enter the gates, they were halted by a soldier. At the same moment, they heard the music of a flute, and a company of the Companions rode forth on prancing horses, followed by a band of foot soldiers.

"Is there a war?" questioned Nearchus of his father.

"No," replied Parmenion with a smile. "They are only

drilling. You will grow accustomed to such sights in Pella. Philip drills his men like a Spartan,—but fortunately he does not feed them upon the Spartan black broth."

When the company had passed, Parmenion and Nearchus entered the gate. The size of the castle and the strength of its walls struck Nearchus with amazement. The courtyard seemed filled with boys, horses, men—all darting, prancing, hallooing. Nearchus' blood went tingling through his veins. "There will be plenty of excitement in life at court," was his thought.

A moment later, he was following his father through the great doors of the palace. For a few moments, he was left alone, and he spent the time in looking about him, and noting the splendor by which he was surrounded.

His own home, near the foothills, was comfortable, but simple in all its appointments. It had seemed to him quite luxurious, however, in contrast to the homes of the people of the hill tribes beyond them. But of such magnificence as he now beheld, he had never dreamed.

The walls about were hung with tapestries of rich, even gorgeous colorings, and they were heavy with the glittering threads of their embroideries. On the floors were soft rugs into which his feet sank as he stepped, and he half drew back, wondering that such beauty should be placed beneath men's feet.

"FOR A FEW MOMENTS HE WAS LEFT ALONE."

On the walls about him hung armor of wonderful workmanship. There were helmets with waving plumes, shields of brass, curiously and richly embossed, and bows so large and heavy it seemed to Nearchus that only a giant could draw them.

Every object upon which he looked was in striking contrast to the simplicity of the Macedonian homes that he had seen. Then he remembered to have heard his father say that Philip had spent many years of his life in Thebes, a city of Greece, and that he had adopted many of the Greek customs, as well as the Greek manner of living.

"I am to learn to speak Greek," thought Nearchus, "and to live like a Greek, it seems. But, all the same…" and he drew himself up to his full height, "I am a Macedonian!"

"Of what are you thinking?" asked a frank, half-amused voice at his side. Nearchus turned. A young boy of about his own age stood before him, and as Nearchus looked upon him, he thought him the most beautiful, the most attractive youth he ever had seen.

With a frankness quite equal to that of his questioner, Nearchus replied, "I was thinking of the new life I am to begin at court. It seems to me that it must be more Greek than Macedonian; and I am a Macedonian!"

The soft eyes of his companion sparkled, and he thrust out his hand. "I, too, am a Macedonian," said he, as he grasped Nearchus' hand in a cordial clasp, "but you know we Macedonians are also Greeks."

"We are Greeks?" questioned Nearchus, looking puzzled.

"Yes, indeed we are, of the same race, the same stock. I will prove it to you some day, but now I must hurry on. I am late at the gymnasium already, and Leonidas is very strict." He made a wry face; then, with a laugh and a friendly nod, he was gone.

"Well," exclaimed Parmenion,—and Nearchus turned at sound of his father's voice,—"you have made the acquaintance of Alexander early!"

"Alexander!" exclaimed Nearchus. "Was that Alexander? I did not know!" Then he added, "But I might have known no other boy could have such beautiful features and so noble a bearing."

As he followed his father through what seemed endless halls and chambers, he kept repeating under his breath, "Alexander! Alexander! And he was the first person in Pella to greet me!"

Nearchus had been so amazed by his meeting with the young prince that he had given no thought to the ordeal of being presented to the King. But in spite of the luxury and grandeur of the castle and its furnishings, Philip cared comparatively little, when among his own intimates, about ceremonials and forms. He was on good terms with his Companions, and the presentation of their sons as Pages was not a very trying ordeal after all.

On the afternoon of the same day, Nearchus found himself, with other boys, ushered into the King's presence. The room was even more magnificent than those which Nearchus had previously seen, and Philip sat upon his throne in his kingly robes.

The father of each boy made a speech, and introduced his son by name to the King. Some of the speeches were rather long and filled with praises of the King. But Parmenion, who chanced to be last, contented himself by saying, "This, oh, King, is my elder son, Nearchus. May he be a loyal subject, and serve you well."

Then the King addressed the boys briefly, ending by charging them to remember that in serving him they served all Macedonia.

Soon after this, they were dismissed, going to the quarters assigned the youths, where they were instructed in their duties by the master of the Pages.

And so, with little ceremony, but with great earnestness of purpose, Nearchus became a Page of King Philip of Macedon.

CHAPTER III

NEW FRIENDS

THE quarters assigned the Pages had none of the luxury of the palace, but to the boys recently come from a simpler home life, they seemed more familiar than the gorgeous furnishings of the court. But they were soon to grow accustomed to the sight of luxury through their daily attendance upon the King.

Antipater, the master of the Pages, gave the boys a brief outline of their new duties. They were, in their turn, to guard at night the door of the King's apartment; they were to take his horse from the groom and to bring it to the King; when the King hunted, some of them would be chosen to accompany him; and when he went into battle, a chosen number would go with him to form his body-guard.

"For these and similar services you will be trained and drilled," said Antipater. "In time we shall look to you for the generals and officers of the Macedonian army, for that is the final object of your training. In the meantime you will have studies to master, military tactics to learn, gymnasium exercises to practice."

After giving the boys some sound advice as to their conduct and general deportment, Antipater dismissed them.

As the boys left the classroom, Nearchus and another of the group, named Aretis, felt their arms grasped in friendly fashion by Lysippus, an attractive youth but little older than themselves. "Come," said he, "let us take a walk together and I will show you about. Antipater says the same things to every new group of Pages," he continued laughingly, "and scares us—at least he does most of us. But it really is not as hard as it all sounds. We manage to have a great deal of fun, and life at court is full of change and excitement.

"There are some things, though, that Antipater fails to tell, but which are good things to know," Lysippus continued, his eyes sparkling with mischief. "For instance, Lysimachus, who is one of Alexander's teachers—and ours as well—can be managed very nicely if one just calls him Phoenix now and then."

"Why is that?" asked Nearchus, entering heartily into Lysippus' mood, and feeling truly thankful to be chosen for his confidences.

"Oh, Phoenix is one of the characters of the Iliad, as

you will find when you begin the study of Greek, and Lysimachus imagines that he resembles him, because he is Alexander's tutor. Lysimachus calls Alexander, Achilles, and Philip, Peleus. The Iliad is his hobby, so, if you like Greek, you can get on with him very well.

"Leonidas, however, is different. He is strict as a Spartan, and not easily fooled. Why, he even goes through Alexander's chests to make sure that Queen Olympia—Alexander's mother, you know—has not given him luxuries of any sort. Leonidas is a relative of Queen Olympia, and so he thinks himself a privileged character. He has general charge of Alexander and the rest of us. One has to be pretty sharp to steal a march on him.

"There are other teachers, but you will learn to know them in class. They are not so important."

"What studies do you have besides Greek?" asked Aretis.

"History, music, and drawing," replied Lysippus.

"Drawing!" exclaimed Aretis, with shining eyes. "Oh, but I am glad! I would rather learn to draw and to paint than to do anything else I know of."

Lysippus' eyes were shining too, as he held out his hand to Aretis. "Here is my hand on that!" he exclaimed. "Only I want to be a sculptor, rather than a painter."

The two boys clasped hands warmly. "I hardly dare

to say among the boys that I would rather chisel than fight," Lysippus continued, "for they all are eager to lead soldiers into battle, and I would not want them to think me a coward. But I was named for the great sculptor, Lysippus, and I trust that I may not prove altogether unworthy of the name."

"I can understand," said Aretis earnestly, "for I, too, love art. Yet probably most of the boys would not."

Nearchus had listened to this conversation with interest. He knew little about art. His father was his ideal, and the life of the soldier and the officer was the only life of which he had been taught.

"But I think that Alexander understands," Lysippus continued, "for though he is every inch a soldier himself, he admires both poets and artists."

The boys soon after separated, but between Lysippus and Aretis a lasting bond had been formed.

The days that followed were busy days for the new Pages of Philip's court. It seemed to Nearchus that he had entered a new world, so entirely was his life changed.

For a part of each day he was to be seen darting here and there about the court, carrying messages for one or another of the Companions and officers. Certain hours of the day were devoted to lessons, others to gymnastic

"CERTAIN HOURS OF THE DAY WERE DEVOTED
TO... GYMNASTIC AND MILITARY DRILL."

and military drill, and between these busy hours there were times when he was left to his own devices.

He had learned quickly the plans of the palace and its outer courts, as well as the names of the prominent men who came and went, and he was soon known as one of the most alert and willing messengers of the court.

He readily became acquainted with those who, like himself, had just entered the King's service, and among these Aretis was one of his favorites. The older boys were as a rule inclined to hold aloof, and some of them thought it fun to tease the new arrivals. Lysippus, however, was always friendly.

"Come," said Aretis to Nearchus, one day, "we have finished our lessons. Let us go and watch the games. I have heard that the King, himself, is to wrestle in the arena."

Away the boys sped, fleet of foot as two young deer. As they turned a corner they came into sudden collision with an older boy named Philotas, whom they had seen about the palace.

Nearchus was knocked, half-breathless, into the street. In a moment, however, he scrambled to his feet and looked, half laughingly, into Philotas' face. But the scowl which he met was anything but friendly.

"Oh," exclaimed Nearchus frankly, "I did not intend

to be so hasty as all that." He spoke, as usual, in the Macedonian dialect, for he had not yet mastered the Greek well enough to venture to speak it.

"Keep your Macedonian tongue for the soldiers," exclaimed Philotas contemptuously. "I speak Greek."

"And how long have you spoken Greek, Philotas? Nearchus' *manners* at least are Greek."

The questioner had come up unobserved. His tone was one of intense scorn. But at the sound of his voice, Nearchus turned quickly, and his cheeks flushed, for he knew that it was the voice of Alexander.

Philotas' dark cheeks flushed, too, but not with pleasure, though he tried to answer lightly, "The young rascal nearly knocked my breath out."

"I saw it," said Alexander. "We will have to put him in training for the foot-races soon. But come," he added, "were you bound for the arena? If so, come with me and I will see that you have good seats."

He had included them all in his invitation, and swinging about, they walked off together.

Nearchus felt as though treading on air, as he walked by Alexander's side to the arena; but he did not know how many of the boys of Pella looked upon him with envious eyes as he sat by Alexander's side during the games. Neither did he know it then—although he guessed it afterward—that thenceforth no boy among them would dare treat him with disrespect. If Alexander had chosen him for a friend, that settled the matter for every loyal boy in Pella.

CHAPTER IV

THE GAMES

THE games of the arena were intensely interesting, especially to the boys who had so recently come to the city and to whom they were wholly new.

There were foot-races first, and it seemed to Nearchus that the young men who took part in them must, like the god Hermes, have wings upon their feet. He had never seen such swiftness, such lightness in running; and when the victor was crowned, he shouted lustily with the others, "Io, pæan!"[1] for that much Greek he had learned.

The foot-races were followed by wrestling. Several contests took place between youths, and then between older men. Then there was deep silence for a moment, followed by a thunderous shout of applause, as Philip, King of Macedon, stepped into the arena.

His opponent was a powerful man, and for a time the two seemed well matched, but Philip was quicker in motion, and in the end his opponent was thrown. Then

---

1   " Io, pæan" (To, pē'an) a shout of victory.

again rang the "Io! Io! pæan!" till it seemed to echo back from the very skies above them.

When Philip left the arena wearing the wreath of victory, he bore himself quite as proudly as when he wore his kingly crown of gold.

This was the last event of the day, and the seats surrounding the arena were soon emptied.

As the boys regained the street, they were joined by another group.

"Come," said Alexander, "we have been sitting so long, let us have a foot-race and see who will reach quarters first."

Away they all darted. But it could hardly be called a foot-race, for the crowds and the narrow crooked streets made swift running out of the question. They ducked here, and doubled there, dashed ahead when they found a few feet of clear space, or made a detour when they found a street blocked by the throng. It became a contest of dexterity and adroitness, rather than of speed. No two had taken the same course.

When Nearchus reached quarters, quite out of breath but glowing with the exercise, he looked about for the other boys. None were in sight. "I must have made a mistake as to where we were to finish," he thought. But no, for there was Alexander dashing toward him, and from different directions the other boys were coming. There was Ptolemy, Aretis, Charias, Harpalus, Amyntas, Lysippus: one after another they came running in, laughing, panting, breathless, until all who had started in the race were there. No, all but one—Philotas had not yet come.

"Nearchus won the race!" cried Alexander.

"Oh, but 'twas no race," declared Nearchus modestly. "It was just a game of duck and dodge."

"Well," insisted Alexander, "you won, in any case. But where is Philotas?" he added.

The boys looked about. They were sure he would come, for he had started with the others, and it was now almost time for their drill.

"Here he is," cried Aretis at length. "But look! What has befallen him?"

As the boys turned, they saw Philotas making his way slowly toward quarters. He walked with a slight limp. His lip was cut, and in rubbing it he had covered his face half over with blood. It was no wonder that the boys gathered about him and together asked, "What has happened?"

"Oh," said Philotas, his swollen lip making the Greek speech of which he boasted sound somewhat thick, "I found myself back of a burly soldier, and tried to duck past him, but just as I would have shot by, he stepped directly in front of me. I couldn't stop, and we both went down. He was on top and naturally he got up first; and then he set upon me like a big brute. By Hermes! I couldn't help tripping him!"

Alexander turned away. There was an amused smile upon his face as he did so. Nearchus and Aretis exchanged laughing glances.

Philotas saw it. He also saw Alexander's smile; and a sudden red, which was not the red from his bleeding lip, rose to the roots of his hair. Till that moment he had forgotten his encounter with Nearchus.

CHAPTER V

IN BARRACKS

"**W**HAT have you there, Alexander?"

The boys had gathered, after their evening meal, around one of the flaring lamps of the barracks; all but those who, at this hour, were in attendance upon the King.

Alexander, who was oftener in barracks than in the palace, held in his hand a gold coin.

"It is a gold stater," he replied. "I wanted to show it to Nearchus."

Nearchus turned in surprise.

"Do you remember, Nearchus," Alexander continued, "of my telling you that some time I would prove to you that we Macedonians are also Greeks?"

"Yes," answered Nearchus quickly, "I do remember."

"Look here," continued Alexander, and Nearchus bent his head over the shining gold stater.

"Father had these coins stamped to celebrate the victory of his horses in the Olympic games. They won the race in the year that I was born."

The boys crowded closely about to examine the engraved figures upon the coin, while Alexander continued:

"Now, you all know, of course, that none but a Greek can take part in great games at Olympia. We are Macedonians, but we are of Greek stock. The guardians of the games have so declared it. Indeed, we are of purer Greek blood than most of the Athenians or Corinthians, for they have mingled more with other nations and intermarried with them."

"I knew that the King had won some of the Olympic races," said Nearchus thoughtfully, "and still I had not thought before of our being of Greek blood. Yet I know that heavy penalties follow if one who is not a Greek takes part in the games. They must, in fact, take oath that they are Greek before they can enter."

"I wonder what Macedonian first won a prize at Olympia," said Lysippus. "Who knows?"

"I believe it was King Alexander," said Ptolemy, "about one hundred years ago. And Pindar, the Greek poet, wrote some verses about his victory."

"Ask Ptolemy, every time, if you want any facts from history," said Alexander.

"But if you want a quotation from Homer," retorted

Ptolemy, "ask Alexander. He sleeps with his Iliad under his head."

"Yes," added Lysippus, "and knows a good share of it by heart."

"'Tis true," assented Alexander, "and I shall know all of it by heart before I finish. Perhaps the Odyssey, too."

Charias and Philotas groaned. "If I learn enough of Homer to satisfy Lysimachus, *I* shall be satisfied," said Philotas. "But he thinks we should all study Greek as Alexander does. I would rather learn to box and wrestle."

"I like to hunt, and to play ball," said Alexander, "but I do not like boxing or wrestling."

"You are a good runner," said Charias. "Would you take part in a foot-race at Olympia if you could?"

"I would if I could have kings for competitors," replied Alexander tersely.

Later, when Alexander had left them, the boys continued their talk.

"Why does Lysimachus so often call Alexander, Achilles?" asked Nearchus.

"Because he would have Alexander pattern after the hero of the Iliad," replied Ptolemy, "as indeed he does. Achilles is Alexander's ideal. And, besides, you know it is commonly said that Alexander is descended from the gods, even as Achilles was."

"Well," cried Nearchus, "whether Alexander is descended from the gods, I know not; but one thing I do know — he is every inch a king!"

"'Tis true; 'tis true!" responded the boys heartily.

"But it takes Nearchus to defend him," laughed Ptolemy.

"He needs no defense!" replied Nearchus warmly.

"Well, at any rate, he has a good champion in you," insisted Ptolemy, who liked to tease, even though he admired Nearchus.

"We are all his champions!" declared Nearchus stoutly.

"Yes, yes! Good, good!" responded the boys again, and only Aretis noticed that Philotas did not join in the shout.

But the noise had attracted the attention of Leonidas, whose strict ideas of discipline made little allowance for boyish fun or enthusiasm.

He walked over to the group. "Less noise!" he commanded, "and off to your beds." Then he added, "You will need to sleep. Tomorrow night some of you are likely to be on the march."

The boys turned in quickly, but exchanged low-toned comments before dropping off to sleep.

"What does Leonidas mean?" questioned Lysippus.

"I heard that couriers arrived today, and were with the King for a long time," said Ptolemy.

"Does it mean that there is to be war?" asked Nearchus.

"The couriers might bring any sort of news," answered Ptolemy, "but in what Leonidas just said I can see no other meaning."

CHAPTER VI

IN CAMP

THE following day was filled with tense excitement for the boys. It became known that Philip had for some time been planning in secret an attack upon a rebellious city, and had only awaited the coming of his couriers for an immediate start.

His soldiers were so thoroughly organized, and so constantly drilled and exercised in the maneuvers of war, that they were ready to march on the shortest notice.

The King's body-guard was selected from among the older Pages. The others were kept busy darting here on this errand, there on that, as the King or his generals gave quick command.

The fathers of many of the Pages were among the generals who were to accompany the King. Parmenion was one of these.

The quarters of the common soldiers were on the plains outside the walls of Pella, and the boys were glad whenever a message from the King took them there. There were hundreds of tents spread wide over the plain.

Horses were neighing and prancing, generals in their uniforms were riding to right and left, giving orders; the soldiers were packing the provisions and arms which they were to carry. Wagons were being loaded with the munitions of war; metal trimmings and pieces of armor were being polished. In every direction there were flying colors, the music of flutes, all the movement and life and subdued excitement of a great army preparing for a march.

As Nearchus and Aretis were leaving the camp, after delivering messages there, they saw Philip approaching with his body-guard.

Heralds rode in advance, and the shrill sound of martial music both startled and thrilled the boys. The King was coming to inspect the camp.

As Philip approached, the great mass of the foot soldiers shouted in unison a salutation in the Macedonian dialect, then together they struck upon their shields with their heavy pikes, in sign of their readiness for battle.

Nearchus and Aretis stood "at attention" as Philip and his escort rode by. The Pages who formed the King's body-guard were dressed in holiday attire. Their tunics were of purple — the royal color. On their feet were sandals, and over their shoulders hung short cloaks of richly embroidered patterns.

As the boys stood watching, they heard a familiar voice beside them. They turned and faced Parmenion. He was dressed in full military costume and rode a magnificent black horse. On his head was a helmet of metal, his body was covered with a cuirass of leather thickly covered with metal scales, and his feet and legs were incased in high leather boots. A blanket sufficed for saddle. When he went into battle he would carry a short, straight, two-edged sword, and a lance of wood, metal tipped.

"Stay in the field for a time," he said to the boys. "The phalanx is to be formed under Philip's direction. It will be worth while for you to see it."

The boys were glad to obey, for the phalanx, as formed and drilled under Philip, was known and dreaded wherever the Macedonian army marched. The boys had heard much about it, but never yet had had an opportunity of seeing it.

At a command from Philip, each man who belonged to this body of the troops grasped his weapon, a lance of wood, eighteen feet in length, tipped with metal. Each held his lance with his left hand, about four feet from its end, and supported the longer portion with his right. They formed in close ranks, with the points of their lances thrust forward. In this way the lance points of all but the last row reached beyond the men of the first. Truly it was a formidable hedge of bristling metal with which to charge an enemy's lines.

"Who could stand against it?" cried Aretis, but even as he spoke he turned away, for the sight did not arouse in him a feeling of exultation, as it did in Nearchus.

"Splendid!" shouted Nearchus, watching now the movements of the phalanx, now those of his father, who rode across the field at Philip's side. "Oh, I wish I were one of the Pages to go with the King. What a charge they will make!" For Nearchus had been taught of war all his life, and his father was his model and hero.

But Aretis had the instincts of the artist rather than those of the soldier. To himself he said, "I have thought I was a true Macedonian — yes, and I am! — but I fear I am no soldier; for though I trust I should do my duty if I had to go into battle, I could never want to see a charge of the phalanx, as the other boys do."

He was glad to turn from the bristling line of lance points to watch a body of light-armed foot soldiers who were marching in another part of the field. These were armed with a long sword, a lance, and a shield; and Aretis watched with interest their swift motions as they drew up in line and went through their drill of attack and of quick defense with their shields.

"That, to me, seems fairer," he said to Nearchus. "The phalanx is too much like butchery."

"That may be," responded Nearchus slowly; but he realized that what he had once heard Aretis say was true — few of the boys of Macedonia could understand the way Aretis felt about war.

It is not to be understood that the blood of both the boys did not tingle at sound of the martial music, the sight of glittering uniforms, the position and adroitness of the military movements. They would not have been human boys if it had not. But beneath and beyond the stirring spectacle of the camp, Aretis saw, in his own mind, the bloody scenes of the actual battle, and from these his whole being recoiled.

But Nearchus could not look at it from the same standpoint. He was a soldier, as was his father, as was almost every boy and man of Macedonia, and all his training had been the soldier's training, which fostered love of conquest and eagerness for the excitement of battle.

Nearchus was a brave, typical Macedonian boy, living at a time when "peace had had no achievements worthy of record."

The two boys were unusually silent as they walked back side by side. Aretis was wishing that Lysippus had been with him, instead of Nearchus. "I wonder whether he would have looked upon all the scenes of the camp as Nearchus does, and as all the other boys do. I cannot believe that he would," he said to himself. "I think that he would have understood me."

Nearchus' thoughts returned to his father, and he glowed with pride as he remembered how splendid he looked, and how well he rode. And he was filled with impatience for the time when he should be chosen to go into battle with the King.

CHAPTER VII
A FEAST

AFTER Philip and his army had marched away, the boys of Pella found it hard to settle down to the quiet routine of daily lessons and drills. They were ready to welcome any diversion which promised either fun or adventure.

It was with special glee, therefore, that Nearchus, Aretis, Lysippus, Ptolemy, and Charias received a mysterious message from Alexander, bidding them meet him late that evening in a certain room of the palace "with appetites well whetted."

The time set was an hour later than their regular time for being in bed, and the problem of slipping away from their quarters unseen and gaining an entrance to the palace was one of sufficient difficulty to give zest to their appetites both for fun and feasting.

"He is planning a feast, I am certain," said Ptolemy. "Very likely Lanice, his old nurse, has sent it to him. She likes to humor him as well as she did when he was six; and she knows what Spartan-like fare Leonidas allows."

"A feast of Lanice's preparing is worth running many risks to share," added Lysippus.

"You have tasted them before, then?" inquired Aretis.

"Only once," replied Lysippus, "but it is not easily forgotten. One of the boys was caught at that time," he added, "and he received a double dose of both Greek and mathematics as a punishment. But it would have gone worse with him had Leonidas caught him, instead of Lysimachus."

That night, when the flaring lights in the Pages' quarters were extinguished, each boy was in his usual place. But as the quiet of the room grew deeper, and the sound of breathing grew more steady and regular, five figures slipped, one by one, from their beds and stole quietly out into the night.

Each one, taking his own time and course, slid along through the shadows and close to the walls, till he reached a well-known door in the rear of the palace. Here he uttered a single word, "guard" — the pass-word given him by Alexander — and at once the door was opened and softly shut again. Alexander was a favorite with the soldiers and guards about the palace, and a word or two from him, perhaps accompanied by a coin, secured him many a service in his larks.

The palace had become as familiar to the boys as their

"HE REACHED A WELL-KNOWN DOOR
IN THE REAR OF THE PALACE"

own homes, and, once admitted, they had no trouble in following the dark passages to the room which Alexander had designated. A repetition of the pass-word, softly uttered, opened to them the door of this room.

"But where is Ptolemy?" asked Alexander somewhat anxiously after all the others had gathered. No one knew. But a moment later there was a soft tap on the door accompanied by a whispered "guard," and Ptolemy was admitted.

He was breathless and bursting with suppressed laughter.

"What happened to you?" questioned Alexander.

"Oh," exclaimed Ptolemy, as soon as he could speak, "I was feeling my way along a wall in the court when I stumbled over a figure lying on the ground. I thought it one of you boys who had scented danger and dropped to keep from being seen. So, to find out, I said 'guard.' Then you should have heard the fellow! He was evidently one of the soldiers on duty, and had fallen asleep. When I said 'guard' he thought I was about to summon an officer of the guard and have him imprisoned. He begged and implored me not to do it, and promised by all the gods of Macedonia never to fall asleep at his post again.

"Well, you may imagine I was glad to quiet him with

a promise, and I left him calling down all the blessings of Olympus on my head."

"'Twas a narrow escape," laughed Alexander. "We would have been sorry to have our feast without you."

"And I would have had greater cause for sorrow than you," replied Ptolemy, as he saw the store of good things which Alexander was rapidly bringing forth.

There were honey cakes, figs, dates, everything in fact that the skill and the purse of Lanice could supply, or the appetite of a Macedonian boy could demand.

"What a nurse to have!" cried Lysippus.

The boys did full justice to the feast, talking at the same time of Philip's expedition; of his plans for uniting the forces of Greece with his own; and from that to the games and wrestling matches of the gymnasium.

At last, unwillingly, they took leave of Alexander, going as they had come, one by one.

Nearchus had slipped safely back to his bed, and was wondering whether the others had succeeded as well as he, when he became conscious of a light above him. He opened his eyes — too readily, as he immediately realized — and looked up into the face of Leonidas.

No word was said, but the light was carried to the next bed, and the next, until the round of the quarters had been made. Then it was extinguished.

"I wonder if all the boys were back!" exclaimed Nearchus to himself. "Well, Leonidas evidently suspected something, and now I suppose we are in for it!"

He wondered what their punishment would be, for he knew that Leonidas was strict — strict as a Spartan — and that something was bound to follow such an infringement of rules. But it was late, and so, wondering, he fell asleep.

CHAPTER VIII

AN ALL-NIGHT TRAMP

PERHAPS Leonidas had a grim sense of humor.

Nothing was said in class the next day about an infringement of rules. No one was called before the master and reprimanded. No one was even questioned.

But when the recitations were over, Leonidas addressed them. "It is perhaps natural," he began, "with the King on the battlefield and a part of our number accompanying him, that there should be a feeling amongst us of restlessness, and a spirit of adventure and daring."

If a half-dozen of the boys before him wondered what was to follow they dared not betray it by the exchange of a single glance.

"While this feeling may be natural," continued Leonidas, "it is not in harmony with studious application. Therefore—" Leonidas paused long enough to make his announcement duly impressive — "we will start this evening on an all-night tramp. This, I believe, will serve to satisfy the spirit of adventure, and to make us value our beds at night."

And with that they were dismissed.

"Upon my word, but we got off easy!" exclaimed Nearchus, as he met Lysippus later. "But Leonidas knows all about our adventure last night. You may depend upon that!"

"There is no doubt of it," responded Lysippus.

"I thought we would be well punished," chuckled Nearchus.

"No one but the King is permitted to punish a Page," said Lysippus. "However, we may not think ourselves so fortunate by the time we finish our all-night tramp!"

"That is true," assented Nearchus. "I must confess, though, that I am eager for it. At least," he added with a laugh, "I should be if I were not so sleepy!" Since Nearchus had come from his home near the hills to the court at Pella, he had wished many times that he might climb the hills again, forgetting drills and studies and restraints. Now he was to have a tramp into the country in all likelihood; and so to him the threatened form of punishment seemed altogether attractive. But he forgot that he was reckoning without his host.

Many times had Leonidas been likened by the boys of Pella to a Spartan, but never did he better deserve the comparison than during their adventure of that night. Leaving Pella at dusk, the company of some twenty or more boys first marched for miles over level ground; then they forded a shallow river. After that their way led across foothills till they reached a spur of a mountain range.

Here they had to climb over rocks and up steep slopes; they swam across a rapid stream whose waters were as cold as they were rapid. Scrambling out upon the opposite bank, they again climbed steep and rugged surfaces till the strain upon their muscles caused the blood to run tingling through their veins. Reaching the height at last, they raced down a long slope, then resumed their steady march over level ground, until—just as dawn began to break, they saw before them the walls of Pella.

Then they cheered!

The breakfast which they found ready for them when they reached quarters tasted as good as a royal banquet, and Lysippus whispered to Nearchus that he believed Lanice herself had cooked it.

If the boys had hoped for an hour's sleep before beginning the day's duties, they were disappointed. Classes met as usual, exercises in the gymnasium followed, and military drill filled the greater part of the afternoon, ending with a lesson in drawing.

"Will the day never end?" yawned Aretis.

"It would seem not," grinned Nearchus. "Leonidas is giving us our medicine!"

"Pshaw!" exclaimed Ptolemy, "he is only teaching us to endure hardship. Wait till we are soldiers and we will laugh at this." Then, suddenly dropping his tone of assumed superiority, he added with a shrug, "But I shall need no god of slumber to coax my eyelids shut tonight!"

After the drawing class, Aretis convulsed the boys who had taken part in Alexander's feast by showing them a hasty but unmistakable sketch of Leonidas, lamp in hand, peering down into the sleeping face of a boy who was no less unmistakably Nearchus.

He was about to destroy the sketch when Alexander caught it from his hand.

"'Tis too good to destroy! Let me keep it!" he exclaimed.

Then, as he examined it again, he looked earnestly into Aretis' eyes. "The likeness is truly remarkable," he said. "I did not know you were so good an artist. When I am King, Aretis, I shall send you to the studio of the great Apelles to study painting."

"I shall remember that," answered Aretis quietly. "It will suit me better than fighting."

CHAPTER IX

A STORY OF THE SEA

IT was several months after Philip's army had left Pella that a courier came riding into the city bearing news of a great victory. There had been a long siege, but at last the walls of the defense had been broken down and the Macedonians had conquered.

There was great rejoicing in Pella, and the people gathered about the market-place and the temples to discuss the details of the siege, as the courier had told them.

The King's Pages were among the most eager of the listeners.

"Philip will yet subdue all Greece," declared Ptolemy. "And, when he has done that, he will combine the Greek army with the Macedonian, and there will be no end to his conquests."

"Yes," exclaimed Alexander somewhat impatiently, turning to the group of boys, "father will get everything in advance. He will leave no victories for me to share with you! How soon does my father expect to return?" he asked of the courier.

"Within a few days," was the reply.

The news soon spread throughout the city, and the quiet routine into which the city's life had settled was again broken by active preparations for receiving the victors.

But the courier's news was not of unmingled gladness. He brought with him the list of those whose lives had been lost in battle, and in more than one house in Pella the doors were closed against the sounds of rejoicing in the streets, while those within mourned for the one who would not return with the victors.

Nearchus had listened with a fast beating heart as the list of names was read, and when it was finished and he knew that his father was safe he could scarcely speak for joy.

That evening a group of boys gathered about a soldier named Attalus, who was a member of the palace guard. During the day it chanced that Charias had overheard him telling a comrade about an adventure he had once had at sea. Charias immediately told the other boys, and they had begged Attalus to tell them something of his life on the water. As Alexander was among their number, the soldier felt flattered by the notice he was receiving, and he told his story well.

At that time Macedonia had no sea-coast, for although the Ægean Sea was little more than twenty miles south from Pella, yet all the coast was occupied by Greek settle-ments. So the boys of Macedonia knew as little about the water as though it had been two hundred miles away instead of twenty. But it had then, as it always has, a fascination all its own, and the boys listened eagerly and asked many questions.

"What are the war vessels like?" questioned Alexander.

"They are triremes," said Attalus: a vessel with three decks of oars. The rowers are picked for their strength and endurance, as well as for their dexterity, for it is often necessary to make quick and sudden shifts of action. Sometimes one ship will be sent head-on against another, almost cutting it in two; or it will be sent alongside, breaking the oars on one side of the ship it is attacking. When it cuts into an enemy's boat, it must back away immediately or it will be boarded by the enemy and a hand-to-hand battle follow. To avoid this, the rowers must be ready to reverse their stroke instantly, when the signal is given."

"How is it possible for the men to manage so many oars at one time?" asked Nearchus.

"The rowers are seated on benches in three tiers, on each side of the ship, with an opening alongside for every oar," replied Attalus. "There is always an oar master to keep the time for them. He strikes a metal instrument, or he plays a flute, and sometimes the men sing, but always they keep time to the music with the stroke of the oars."

"But do they never rest?" exclaimed Lysippus.

"Oh, yes; they have extra rowers to relieve them, turn about. Sometimes, too, there is a favorable wind. Then the sails are set, and the men stop rowing. One man is always at the rudder to steer the boat.

"It was on the Mediterranean Ocean that I had my most exciting adventure. I was not at that time on a man-of-war, but on a merchantman. The merchantmen have fewer oars, usually one bank, as ours had, so it moves much more slowly than a man-of-war.

"We usually kept close to shore, for there were plenty of pirate ships looking for booty. We had a valuable cargo on board, of spices and silks, and we had no mind to lose it."

Every boy in the circle was listening intently, but presently Nearchus received a nudge from Alexander's elbow. Alexander did not speak as Nearchus looked at him, but merely nodded in the direction of another of the group. It was Philotas. He was leaning forward, his lips parted, his eyes gleaming with the intensity of his interest. He had forgotten everything but the story of Attalus. He was drinking in every word.

Nearchus exchanged an understanding, half-amused

glance with Alexander, and then both turned their attention once more to the soldier's narrative.

"But one night a storm caught us. It was from off
shore, and drove us out to sea. In the morning, when
the wind had gone down, we tried to get our bearings,
but could see no land in any direction. Suddenly a speck
appeared, but it was not land. It grew larger, and we saw
that it was another boat. Then, as it came nearer, we
became certain that it was a pirate craft.

"The men at our oars rowed for life, but the merchantman was not only more heavily built, but it carried a
large cargo, and the light craft of the pirate gained upon
us rapidly.

"We were so intent upon watching our pursuers that
no one looked in any other direction. Then we were
startled by a shout. Some one had discovered another
vessel. It, too, was coming in our direction, and as we
looked it seemed a very monster of the sea… such a
monster as sailors love to tell about. But it was a trireme; a
man-of-war. How it came to be there no man knew, but
we felt as though the gods themselves must have sent it.

"The captain had discovered our plight, and he headed
straight for the pirate ship. The crew on that vessel was
thrown into confusion by so unexpected a change in
the situation, and the men lost control of their oars. In

another moment the great man-of-war had run her prow through the side of the boat, cutting it in two as with a knife.

"We were saved. But it was a mighty narrow escape. The captain of the man-of-war gave us our bearings, and within a few hours we were again in sight of the coast."

The tense look upon the faces of the boys relaxed as Attalus finished his story — all but Philotas. The look of eager interest remained upon his face, though his eyes seemed still to be looking upon the sea.

As the group broke up, Alexander and Nearchus noticed that Philotas followed the soldier.

After that, whenever Philotas had an opportunity he sought out Attalus and begged for other stories of the sea, and the boys noticed and laughed at the persistence with which he dogged the soldier's steps.

Nearly a month passed. Then, one morning as the classes formed for drill, one boy was missing. Philotas had disappeared.

CHAPTER X

THE KING RETURNS

"WHAT has become of him?"

"Where do you suppose he is?"

A dozen such questions were asked by the boys after a thorough search had been made of the palace, the barracks, and of all the usual haunts of the boys, for the missing Philotas.

"I believe I could make quite a safe calculation," said Alexander.

"And I," added Nearchus.

"What is it? Where do you think he is?" chimed in a dozen voices.

"'Tis my belief he has run away to the sea," said Alexander positively.

"I feel sure of it," added Nearchus, with equal certainty.

"Why—" began Ptolemy, and then he stopped.

Like a flash it came to all the boys: Philotas' interest in the story the guard had told; his devotion to Attalus since that time; his lack of attention to recent lessons and drills; his absence for the last few days from all their sports and pleasures. All these things came to them now, though before they had hardly been noticed, for Philotas was not a favorite among them, and no one had cared especially about his absence, or had given any real thought to the change which had taken place in him.

"We must tell Leonidas," said Nearchus. "He seems to have no idea what has happened to him."

"We must," assented Alexander. "Charias," he added, "you are on duty at the palace the next hour. Leonidas is there. Find him and tell him what we suspect. He will send soldiers and they will soon overtake Philotas. Foolish fellow, to think he could get away!"

"I'll get a catechizing from Leonidas if I do," responded Charias. "But if he asks me too many hard questions I'll send him to you." So, with a laugh, he started toward the palace.

But his message to Leonidas was not delivered. Before he had reached the court of the palace a courier, covered with dust, his horse covered with foam, rode in through the gates.

"Philip returns!" he cried. "The King comes, with all his army. Make ready to receive him!"

In a twinkling every other interest was forgotten. Officers, left on duty at the court, hastened to assemble their companies. Musicians grasped their instruments. Horses were quickly groomed and mounted. Banners were swung.

A procession was formed and went forth to meet the King. Then through the gates of the city the whole populace poured forth: old men, women, children — none could wait within the walls. Even those who had lost husbands or fathers in the battle went forth with the others to greet the King.

It was a gala time, a great holiday. The people tramped along the dusty road, groups of friends took their stations on knolls along the way and waited. The Pages, mounted, dashed by in their purple tunics and embroidered cloaks.

Presently a great shout went up, followed by the crash of lance points on metal shields.

The King had come.

In advance of the army came the heralds. The people parted and lined the way on either side, where they might watch the triumphant pageant.

A long, long time they stood while there passed before them, first, the King dressed in all the splendor of his royal robes and crown, his chariot of richest metals now hung with garlands of flowers, and as he passed, the people shouted, "Long live Philip of Macedon!" After the King came the Companions; then wagons loaded with rich spoils; captives walking in abject sorrow; the cavalry; artillery; the infantry. Many hours it took for the great procession to pass, and at its close the people trooped after, and so returned to the city.

The soldiers disbanded outside the gates, and once more the great camp of the army was formed on the plain about Pella.

The palace had been made ready to receive Philip and his officers, and that night a great banquet was held, and the Pages were bidden to eat at the King's table. Most of the boys were sons of the returned generals, so the banquet was a reunion as well as a feast.

Stories of the battle were rehearsed, wonders of the country they had passed through were described; the great wealth of the city which had been taken was told. There was music, the playing of flutes and other musical instruments, and singing. It was a new and wonderful scene to Nearchus, and beneath all its gayety and gladness there ran within him a deep feeling of thankfulness as he looked often at Parmenion and thanked the gods for his father's safe return.

It was late when the boys, tired but still excited, turned into their beds, and some time later still when they had grown quiet enough for sleep.

" MANY HOURS IT TOOK FOR THE
GREAT PROCESSION TO PASS."

Suddenly the startled and startling voice of Charias rang out. "May the gods forgive me! I forgot all about Philotas, and my message to Leonidas!"

CHAPTER XI

THE AMBASSADORS
ARE ENTERTAINED

THE next morning a group of the Pages, headed by Alexander, appeared before Leonidas. But it was Charias who acted as spokesman.

"Sir," he began, in his most respectful manner—for he always stood somewhat in dread of the stern disciplinarian, and particularly so on this occasion—"I was to have told you yesterday that we boys have reason to believe Philotas has gone to the sea."

Leonidas seemed startled. Whether it was because he had not thought of the possibility of Philotas' going in this direction, or because he had not thought of Philotas at all, the boys were not informed. But he listened attentively.

"I was on my way to tell you, yesterday, when the courier arrived telling of King Philip's approach. In the excitement I forgot my errand, and thought of it only after I was in quarters last night."

Charias stood erect. He was relieved to have made a clean breast of the affair, and he now waited to learn what dire punishment Leonidas would mete out to him. He would undoubtedly be reported to the King.

"Why do you think he has gone to the sea?" asked Leonidas, apparently overlooking Charias' lapse of memory.

Charias began telling him of the guard's story, and of the way Philotas had listened. Then, as he went on, first one and then another of the boys added a word, remembered an incident, or repeated a bit of conversation, until they were in eager discussion, with Leonidas noting carefully every detail.

At last he rose. "I will see the King at once. He will undoubtedly send a detachment of mounted soldiers to look for the boy. 'Tis an unfortunate affair, and I fear he has too long a start for us to overtake him now, though, if your theory is right, he may yet be found in one of the coast towns." With that he dismissed them.

"Did you ever!" exclaimed Charias when he had gone. "I feel positively weak from surprise. He seemed to overlook my fault entirely."

Alexander laughed. "I would wager a stater that he had not thought of Philotas himself till you reminded him. But there is no use in laying a wager, for the matter could never be determined."

Philip did indeed send soldiers to try to trace Philotas; but when they returned, they had no news of the runaway.

A few days later all Pella was set talking over the arrival of a group of ambassadors from Athens. The men were richly dressed, and their manner and bearing proclaimed them of noble birth.

Later in the day, Aretis, acting in his capacity as Page, approached Alexander. Standing in soldierly attitude he said, "I bear a message from the King."

Alexander at once rose to his feet and stood at attention.

"The King desires your presence in the audience chamber where he has received the ambassadors. He wishes you to bring your harp."

Then, having delivered his message, he added casually, "I think he wants you to help entertain his guests from Athens."

"I will come," said Alexander, giving the military salute. And then he added in his familiar tone, "Good! I have been wanting an opportunity to study those ambassadors ever since they arrived."

When Alexander entered the audience chamber a few moments later, Philip was seated upon his throne in all the richness and dignity of his royal robes. About him were his Companions, his counselors and attendants. The

Pages on duty wore their purple tunics and embroidered cloaks. The room itself was royally furnished.

To Alexander the scene was familiar enough. But to the visiting ambassadors from the free city of Athens, this view of royalty was novel and impressive.

Philip was proud of Alexander, as he well might be, for both in mind and in personality he was a boy of unusual promise.

Alexander first played upon the harp, and then recited a portion of his beloved Iliad. For it was a part of the training of every youth at court to be prepared to entertain their elders when asked.

"Have you a dramatic dialogue that you can give?" asked Philip. "If so, we will send for one of your classmates."

"Send for Nearchus," said Alexander; and again Aretis was dispatched.

Nearchus had made good progress in his mastery of the Greek tongue, but it was with many misgivings that he appeared before Philip and these cultured men of Athens.

The dialogue, however, was given with much earnestness and spirit, and was warmly applauded at its close, although Demosthenes, who was one of the ambassadors, could not refrain from commenting upon the Greek of both Alexander and Nearchus, saying that they still had something of the Macedonian tones and accents, which they should try to correct.

The boys flushed at the criticism, but both had the good sense to see that it was just, and they determined to use their best powers to make as perfect as possible their Greek speech.

To the delight of both the boys, they were allowed to remain and listen to the oratory of the older men. Nearchus paid especial attention to the speech of the Athenians, but Alexander had already begun to take a keen interest in the political plans and schemes of conquest of his father, and to him the questions of politics which arose absorbed his whole attention.

The messages from the citizens of Athens were delivered by Demosthenes and Aeschines, two great orators whose names, after more than two thousand years, are still familiar to students all over the world.

The boys were held spellbound by speech such as they never had listened to before. Their elders were no less fascinated.

The men of Macedonia were men of action rather than of words, and there was no one in Philip's court who could speak as these men spoke. And yet, while they listened in wonder to the eloquence of the ambassadors, they held in a certain contempt a people who were not warriors first and orators afterward.

The King gave respectful attention to the arguments of the ambassadors, and promised to send his own representatives to Athens a little later with a reply.

In the evening a great banquet was given in honor of the guests, and in the morning they left Pella accompanied by an escort of Philip's soldiers.

CHAPTER XII

THE HORSE BUCEPHALUS

"**W**HAT is your hurry, Nearchus?" called Alexander.

"Oh," answered Nearchus, stopping short, "I just saw the grooms taking such a magnificent horse into the field! I want to see it tried. I never saw such a beauty, but he seemed full of fire and extremely hard to manage."

"Wait, and I will go with you," said Alexander. "And here come Lysippus and Aretis. Come with us, boys," he called; "we are going to the field to see a new horse put through his paces. Nearchus thinks him a wonder."

When the four boys reached the field they found Philip already there, with a group of his companions. The horse had been brought to Pella from Thessaly, the boys learned, and was offered to Philip for the sum of thirteen talents, or about one thousand dollars.

He was a magnificent animal, all black except for one white mark which resembled the face of a bull. For this reason he had been given the name of Bucephalus, which means bullhead.

"Stand back!" called the men, as the boys approached,

65

for the horse was plunging and rearing, and seemed wholly unmanageable.

An expert horseman from the royal stables held the horse's bridle, and tried to quiet him with his voice, but each time that he spoke the horse reared and plunged again. It was impossible for the man to mount him.

"He is wholly vicious in temper!" exclaimed Philip, after the man had made repeated attempts to mount him and had utterly failed. "Of what value is his beauty when he cannot be managed or tamed!"

Alexander had watched the scene with fascinated interest, and now he exclaimed, "Oh, but it would be a shame to lose such a horse for want of someone with the power to control him!"

"Do not reproach those who are older than yourself," reproved Philip.

But again Alexander insisted, "But what a magnificent animal he would be if once controlled!"

"And do you think that you could control him better than the most expert horseman in my stables?" asked Philip with a show of sarcasm.

Now Alexander had watched all that was being done in a way that was wholly characteristic of him. He used not only his eyes, but his mind, and he had discovered what he believed to be a mistake on the part of the trainer who held the horse. So, in reply to his father's sarcasm, he said quietly, "I should like to try."

"Ho-ho," laughed Philip, amused and not at all displeased with his son's show of courage. "It would require more than your usual rashness to attempt it."

"But I mean it," replied Alexander steadily.

"What will you pay in case you fail to conquer him?" questioned Philip, still regarding Alexander's plea as a joke.

"I will pay the full price of the horse!" declared Alexander.

The King and his companions laughed, but they stopped suddenly, as the boy stepped out into the field and took the bridle from the hand of the astonished groom.

Immediately Alexander turned the horse face about, so that his own black shadow upon the ground was behind, instead of in front of him. Then with a firm, steady voice he spoke to the animal, and with an equally steady hand he reached out and stroked him.

The men and boys who stood about held their breath in fear and suspense, and no wonder, for they all felt that the King's son was risking his life in a daring, perhaps foolish, adventure.

The high-spirited horse, relieved of the fear of his own shadow, which had previously plunged and danced before him, must have felt the masterful power of the personality of the boy who in a few years would conquer men and nations. Seizing the instant of his advantage, Alexander let his cloak fall quietly to the ground, and sprang with one agile leap to the horse's back.

Like a dart from a full-drawn bow the horse was off, but Alexander—summoning all the mastery of will and of muscle which his gymnasium and military drill had given him—kept his seat, and let the horse have his way.

On and on they sped, while the tense crowd watched, then lost them to view beyond a distant rise of ground.

Not a word was exchanged as they waited, breathless, for the outcome, but Philip felt his whole being thrill at the skill and daring of the boy.

So they stood, hardly moving, watching the spot where horse and rider had disappeared. Then a quivering sigh of relief passed through all the group—they dared not shout—but over the rise of ground came the boy and the horse, no longer galloping in mad fury, but cantering quietly toward them.

So they rode back into the field, the quiet, steady voice of the boy praising the magnificent horse in terms of affectionate endearment, while his steady hand stroked his neck, his side, his great flanks.

Bucephalus was conquered! He had found his master.

As Alexander dismounted, Philip threw his arms about him and with manly tears in his eyes exclaimed, "Now I know that I have a worthy successor! Macedonia will never hold you, my son; but greater kingdoms shall be yours to conquer!"

As the group of men and boys returned to the palace, Nearchus, Aretis, and Lysippus fell back. At first they had no words. The scene had left them speechless.

But such a condition does not last long with boys, and Nearchus' emotion finally burst forth in three words which seemed to express it all. "What a Prince!" he exclaimed.

"Yes," added Aretis, "and what a horse to conquer!"

"They are well matched," said Lysippus. "What a study that would have been for a master sculptor!"

Among the Pages of the palace no other subject was discussed, for it soon became known to them all that Philip had bought the magnificent horse, and had given it to Alexander for his own.

Alexander had been the leader among them before; now he was their hero and idol.

CHAPTER XIII

A NEW TEACHER

"HAVE you heard the news?" asked Nearchus one morning, as he met Aretis and Lysippus on the way to drawing class.

"What news?" responded the boys.

"We are to have a new master: one so learned that I fear we will all stand in awe of him."

"Who is he? Tell us all about him," said Lysippus, throwing his arm across Aretis' shoulder. "You are so close to Alexander you learn all the news first. Were you any other," he added with a laugh, "we should be jealous."

With his ready loyalty Nearchus replied, "Alexander is indeed a royal friend." And then he added, "As to the new master, it is no less a person than the great Aristotle, the philosopher of whom all Greece is proud. He is coming as a special instructor of Alexander, but Philip does not believe in giving the Prince a private education, so there is to be a school at Mieza, just southwest of Pella, and at least a dozen of us are to attend."

"What branches will he teach?" asked Aretis.

"That I do not know yet. But there is an interesting story connected with Philip's hiring of him. It seems that the father of Aristotle was at one time the favorite physician of the Macedonian king. But a few years ago Philip, in one of his wars, entirely destroyed Stagira, the city in which Aristotle and his father lived. Some of the citizens were exiled, others were taken as slaves. All were scattered. But now Philip offers to Aristotle a most unusual gift. He promises to fully restore his native city and rebuild its walls. More than that, he will recall its citizens who were exiled, set free all who were sold into slavery, and send them back to their homes in re-built Stagira. Isn't that a gift worthy of a King!"

"Surely it is," responded the boys warmly. "And all this is done to win Aristotle as a tutor for Alexander?" asked Aretis.

"He is already won," replied Nearchus, "and is to be in Mieza within a few days."

"Is he to take the place of Leonidas?" asked Lysippus.

"I think not," replied Nearchus. "At least Leonidas remains in general control of the boys."

They were about to enter the classroom when Lysippus stopped and touched Aretis' arm. Looking about to see that no one else was near, Lysippus drew forth from his tunic a bit of bronze.

"I would show it to no one but you," he said, as he handed it to Aretis.

It was a bronze coin which Lysippus had pounded flat to destroy its inscription. Then upon the flattened surface he had thrown into relief the figure of a boy mounted upon a horse. The workmanship was surprisingly good, and the figures were full of action and well drawn.

Aretis' face lighted with pleasure as he looked at it.

"Did you do it—alone?" he asked.

"Yes," answered Lysippus. "Do you think it fairly good?"

"Fairly good!" exclaimed Aretis. "I think it remarkably good. Show it to the drawing-master."

But Lysippus shook his head.

"At any rate let me keep it long enough to show to Alexander," begged Aretis, and Lysippus reluctantly gave his consent.

A few days later the boys began their work under the teaching of Aristotle. Their school at Mieza was out of doors among beautiful trees in a spot known as the Grove of the Nymphs. A great marble chair served Aristotle as a seat, but much of the time he taught his pupils while walking with them through the shady paths of the grove. Here he discussed with them the subjects of politics, of literature, of eloquence, and of upright moral

"WALKING WITH THEM THROUGH THE
SHADY PATHS OF THE GROVE."

living. He emphasized the value of noble friendships, of a clean, healthy character, as well as of bodily health and hardihood. He taught them that it was more kingly to conquer self than to subdue an enemy.

In after years Alexander often quoted this saying of Aristotle, and he also said, "My father gave me life. Aristotle taught me how to live."

The boys were taught to reason accurately, and to express their ideas clearly, forcefully, and well.

Music and art were also discussed in these walks in the grove, but Aristotle left to others the technical teaching, while he sought rather to arouse in the boys an appreciation of these subjects, and a feeling for the beautiful in all art.

"What a wonderful teacher Aristotle is!" exclaimed Aretis, as he and Lysippus were returning one day to Pella. "Art has a new meaning to me since I have heard him discuss it. Or rather," he added, "I begin now to understand what before I only felt."

"Yes," replied Lysippus, "I know what you mean. He is indeed a wonderful man. But," he added, the mischievous twinkle coming back into his eyes, "he does not look at all as I had fancied him. I thought he would be tall and commanding in appearance, but he is rather shorter than the average. And then he is so careful in his dress; and he wears as many rings and ornaments as a woman!"

"And what had you expected?" laughed Aretis.

"Oh," admitted Lysippus, joining in the laugh, "I supposed a philosopher was careless about everything except his thoughts."

"Well," chuckled Aretis, "that is only one more of the many wrong impressions Aristotle is uprooting from our minds."

CHAPTER XIV

LATER ON

◆NCE more Philip and his army had left Pella for scenes of war and conquest. But life for the boys who made up the school at Mieza went on with little change. They had grown older; had developed mentally as well as physically during their many months of training under Aristotle.

Alexander had begun to look forward to the time—now near at hand—when he should take an active part in Philip's campaigns. And Nearchus, Ptolemy, and the rest of his companions were almost as eager as he to take their places in the great army of conquest.

They had studied politics under Aristotle; they had been trained in military tactics, and drilled in the maneuvers of war. And war was as the atmosphere of Macedonia. They drew in its spirit with every breath; for military pursuits were regarded as the only worthy occupations of the time. Agriculture, commerce, and the trades were carried on by the common people only. No Macedonian of high rank or birth would trouble himself with these—to him—meaner pursuits. His wealth consisted of vast estates, usually given him by the King in return for his military service.

One of the chief aims of Aristotle's training was to teach the boys to think independently.

Turning, one day, to the son of a minor king, he asked, "When you become King, what will you do for me, your teacher?"

"Ah," announced the youth, "I will have you dine at my table. All in my court shall show you honor."

Turning to another, Aristotle asked, "And what favor will you show to me, when you rule as King?"

"You shall be treasurer of all my wealth," asserted the second quickly, "and my chief counselor."

Then Aristotle faced Alexander. "And now, my son, what will you do for your old teacher when you sit on the throne of your father, Philip?"

And Alexander replied fearlessly, "That is a question for the future to answer. How can I tell what to-morrow may bring? When that day and hour come, then I will give you my answer."

"Well said, Alexander!" declared Aristotle. "Well said! The day shall come when thou shalt be the greatest king of all. World-monarch shall be thy title!"

The boys were startled at Aristotle's outburst. Yet there was no feeling of jealousy aroused by it. Alexander's leadership was too positive to admit the possibility of rivalry. Alexander accepted the statement quietly. But the eyes of Nearchus glowed. "Aristotle is right!" he reflected, and the statement crystallized in his mind into positive conviction. "World-monarch shall be his title!"

There was to be a festival in the afternoon, and an offering, and when classes were dismissed the boys returned as quickly as possible to Pella.

Alexander had been appointed, in his father's absence, to take charge of the ceremonial. Nearchus was his chief attendant.

There were the usual contests of the arena, in running, boxing, and wrestling, and when Alexander stood in all the fresh beauty of his young manhood to award the crowns of victory the people went wild in their applause. The victors in the games had been given no such outburst of acclaim.

As Alexander and Nearchus rode back from the stadium to the temple where offerings were to be made to the gods, Alexander exclaimed, "Were I to have my way, I would award crowns to the tragedians, the musicians, and the singers as well as to the athletes. I like to see our men and boys exercise themselves in feats of strength and endurance, but I care nothing for the athlete who makes it a profession."

"But look," he exclaimed abruptly, pointing to a figure in the crowd they were passing.

The young man toward whom he pointed drew quickly back; but not before Nearchus had seen him.

In a tone of amazement Nearchus muttered, "By all the gods, I believe it was Philotas!"

"No other," responded Alexander. "Yet how changed he is! I fear the sea has used him badly. It will be interesting to hear his story."

"That it will!" ejaculated Nearchus. "You know the sea has always held a fascination for me, in spite of all the sailors' yarns about dragons of the deep, magnetic rocks which draw you to destruction, and terrors never dreamed of on the land. I should like to find out, sometime, what the sea is really like."

"Well," smiled Alexander, "you are quite likely to have a chance some day." And though he said no more, Nearchus felt certain that there was a hidden meaning in the lightly made comment.

The procession halted at the temple. Alexander and Nearchus dismounted and entered. The priest, in his white robes, stood beside the altar, his hand on the head of the animal to be slaughtered as a sacrifice to the god.

The fire on the altar leaped up, and upon it Alexander threw a generous handful of rare spices. The fragrance of the incense filled all the place. But the frugal soul of Leonidas, who stood beside Alexander, rebelled at such wasteful extravagance. Into Alexander's ear he muttered, "You should wait, young man, till you are monarch of the lands where spices grow, before making such bounteous offerings!"

Alexander flushed, and his answer flashed back, "Some day I shall be. In the meantime I will not be niggardly with the gods!"

The procession wound its way back to the music of flutes, and at the gates of the palace the people dispersed.

As Alexander and Nearchus entered the doors, a chorus of soldiers took up the words of a rousing battle hymn to the accompaniment of the flutes.

Alexander started and grasped his sword. Then with a laugh, he let his hand drop; but to Nearchus he declared, "That is the sort of music that stirs my very soul."

CHAPTER XV

A FORETELLING

"PHILOTAS has returned!"

The news spread like wild fire among his former companions.

It is hard to say whether he would have been received back into his former position had not his father been one of Philip's trusted officers. But among the boys it was thought that his experience had undoubtedly been punishment enough for his offense. So once more he was given a place among the Pages, and took up his former life of drill, of service, and of study.

But Philotas remained a subject for much discussion among his companions.

"Will he be punished, think you?" questioned Charias.

"Undoubtedly he will," replied Ptolemy, "but it will not be until Philip returns from the war. Only the King can punish one of his Pages, you know, no matter what the offense may be."

"True," conceded Charias. "I heard one of the soldiers

suggesting that he was likely to receive a lashing on the soles of his feet."

Ptolemy made a wry face. "In that case I am glad I am not in his sandals! But it would seem an appropriate punishment for running away. However, the soldier knows nothing about it."

"No, that is true, of course," assented Charias.

Philotas, as soon as he was reëstablished in his old position, was not at all abashed by his inglorious return. In fact, he seemed to think himself rather a hero in the eyes of the boys, and he sought to strengthen this impression by wonderful tales of the sea. He recounted ad ventures of every imaginable sort, and in each one the part that he played was always highly creditable, if not actually heroic.

A few of the boys were inclined to be impressed by the stories until a soldier, happening to overhear one of the tales, remarked, "He is much more likely to have occupied a rower's bench, and to have witnessed a part of what he describes while plying an oar. The other part is pure fiction."

Alexander overheard the soldier's comment, and remembered it.

The next time he sauntered into barracks, it happened that Philotas was in the midst of a thrilling narrative. He was telling of a mountainous wave, and threw up his hand as he described it. Instantly Alexander reached out and caught his hand. With a quick motion he straightened out Philotas' fingers and looked into his palm. One glance satisfied him.

Philotas, with an expression of fury upon his face, snatched away. But Alexander asked quietly, "What makes your hand so hard and calloused, Philotas? It is not like the hand of a Page."

For a moment Philotas seemed choked with rage. Then he recovered himself enough to go on with his story, but Alexander's question remained unanswered.

A look of amusement went round the circle of boys.

Presently Harpalus drawled, "Alexander, when you become commander of the army, you will have to appoint Philotas admiral of the fleet."

"Philotas my admiral! Bah!" ejaculated Alexander. "But I have already chosen my admiral," he added in an altered tone. "Nearchus loves the sea. But he knows enough to temper his love with judgment and with honor. He is courageous, too, and he is not afraid to oppose me when he thinks I am in the wrong. But he does it to my face — not to my back!" And with that he turned away.

"Alexander hits hard when he hits!" exclaimed Ptolemy, as he and Nearchus went out together. "But he has made an enemy of Philotas, and Philotas is not one to forgive readily.”

“Say not that he has *made* an enemy!” returned Nearchus. “Philotas has always been an enemy of Alexander. He cannot bear to see even the King’s son set above himself. He is too small to appreciate Alexander’s greatness.”

“You are right,” responded Ptolemy. “But what is this about Alexander’s appointing you his admiral?”

“He has spoken of it before,” admitted Nearchus. “I begin to think it is not wholly a jest.”

“It is not a jest,” said Alexander — for unnoticed he had joined them.

“Ah, you mean it!” cried Ptolemy, still uncertain whether the conversation was serious or not. “Then,” he added, “if you have your plans so well laid, pray, what part am I to take?”

“You,” declared Alexander, “will be one of my generals and advisers, and afterward, you are to be the historian of my conquests.”

“Good!” shouted Ptolemy. “Nothing would suit me better! And have you placed us all?” he added.

“Not all,” said Alexander, “but many of you; and I shall the rest, in time. Aretis and Lysippus are to study art. I have as great a respect for an artist as I have for a soldier.

"And I think," added Alexander after a moment, with a gesture half comic, half serious, "that Philotas will be the traitor."

Nearchus and Ptolemy drew in their breath quickly; then they laughed. But no one of them dreamed how soon the half idle words of Alexander would seem to them all like a prophecy.

THE END